DOG ON A BROOMSTICK

JAN PAGE
Illustrated by Nick Price

www.kidsatrandomhouse.co.uk

Also available by Jan Page, and published by Corgi Pups:
DOGNAPPED!
THE CHOCOLATE MONSTER
IT'S NOT FUNNY!

For My Mother

DOG ON A BROOMSTICK
A CORGI PUPS BOOK : 9780552545389

First publication in Great Britain

PRINTING HISTORY
Corgi Pups edition published 1997

19 20

Set in Bembo Schoolbook

Corgi Pups Books are published by Random House Children's Books,
61–63 Uxbridge Road, London W5 5SA,
a division of The Random House Group Ltd

Addresses for companies within The Random House Group Limited
can be found at:
www.randomhouse.co.uk/offices.htm

Printed and bound in Great Britain by
CPI Cox & Wyman, Reading, RG1 8EX

The Random House Group Limited supports The Forest Stewardship
Council (FSC), the leading international forest certification organisation.
All our titles that are printed on Greenpeace approved FSC certified paper
carry the FSC logo. Our paper procurement policy can be found at:
www.rbooks.co.uk/environment

CONTENTS

Series Reading Consultant: Prue Goodwin
Lecturer in Literacy and Children's Books,
University of Reading

CHAPTER ONE

The Witch woke up one night to find her cat had gone. It had left a note on the cat flap.

"I have given up magic," the note read. "I have found a new job, testing cat food."

The Witch was very cross.

She needed a cat to help her with her spells. And there were only three days to go until the Grand Spell Contest!

"Bother! I'll have to find a
new cat," she said.

In the morning, the Witch put
on her tallest hat and went to the
pet shop.

"I want to buy a cat," she told
the shop-keeper.

The shop-keeper did not like the look of the Witch, but he showed her some black kittens in a basket.

"Do they scratch?" asked the Witch.

"No!" said the shop-keeper.

"Do they arch their backs?"
"No!" said the shop-keeper.
"Do they spit and hiss?"
"No!" said the shop-keeper.
"Never!"

"What a shame," said the Witch and walked out of the shop.

Next, the Witch went to the RSPCA. There were lots of cats there, all looking for a new home.

The Witch made them sit in a
row and told them about the job.

"I am looking for a cat to help
me with my spells," she said.
"You will have to catch mice,
spiders and worms. And
sometimes, I might turn you into
a frog. Any questions?"

11

A fat white cat raised her paw.
"Will we have to fly on your
broomstick?"

"Of course!" said the Witch.

"I don't fancy that," said the fat
white cat. "I get airsick."

"Hopeless!" cried the Witch.
She went to see the lady in charge.

"None of these cats are any
good," she told her. "They are
not lean enough. They are not

mean enough. And their eyes
are not green enough!"

"If I found you the right cat,
would you promise to look after
it?" asked the lady.

"Of course not!" said the
Witch. "I want a cat so that it
can look after me!"

The Witch walked out in a temper. Where was she going to find a cat in time for the Grand Spell Contest?

CHAPTER TWO

On her way home the Witch
went to buy some black
chocolates. This gave her a good
idea.

"I know! I'll put a card in the shop window."

The Witch wrote out the words and gave them to the shop-keeper.

Wanted —
Witch's Cat!
Must be able to scratch, hiss and spit.
Only black cats with green eyes need apply.

"That should do it," she said.

The Witch went home and waited. She waited all day and all night but not one cat came.

She was in a panic. Now it was
only two days until the Grand
Spell Contest.

Then, on Thursday evening
there was a scratch at the door.

"At last!" she cried.

She opened the door and saw a
dog sitting on the doorstep.

"Bother!" said the Witch.

"I was hoping you had come about the job."

"I have come about the job," said the Dog.

"But this job is for a cat!" said the Witch.

"That's a bit unfair," replied the Dog. "I am sure I could do the job just as well . . . if not better."

"Don't be stupid!" cried the
Witch. "Witches don't have

dogs. Who ever heard of a
witch's dog?"

But the Dog was not giving up.

"I can fetch and carry. I can hunt. I can bark at strange people."

"But I like strange people," said the Witch. "A lot of my friends are strange people!"

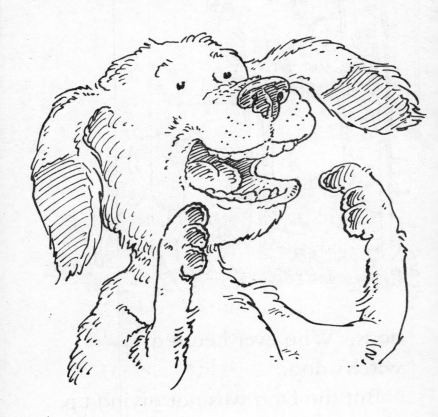

"I will always do as I am told.
I will be the perfect witch's dog.
Please let me try!"

The Dog sat on the doorstep
and wagged his tail. He really
wanted this job. He was so
hungry and cold, he didn't care

what he had to do to find a new home.

The Witch looked him up and down.

"Can you miaow?" she asked.

"No . . . but I can howl at the moon," said the Dog. He opened his mouth and let out a loud, wild howl.

"Ooh, I like that! That sounds very scary!" The Witch smiled and showed her black, crooked teeth.

"Can you hiss and spit?" asked the Witch.

"No . . . but I can growl and dribble," said the Dog. He gave a deep growl and dribbled all over the floor.

"Very good!
What a lovely
mess! . . . Now,
can you arch
your back and
make your fur
stand on end?"

"No . . . but
I can roll over
and leave hair
all over the
carpet," said
the Dog. He
showed her his
best roll.

"That hair could come in handy for my spells," said the Witch, feeling very pleased. "Now I want you to catch a mouse."

The Dog did not know how to catch mice. He found a toy mouse in the old cat's basket and put it between his teeth. The Witch didn't seem to notice.

"Good! Pop it in the cauldron!
. . . Now fetch me some worms
from the garden. Fat ones, or the
spell won't work."

The Dog ran into the garden
and dug a hole. He soon came
back with the fattest worms the
Witch had ever seen.

"Now sit still while I try out this spell on you."

The Dog sat very still.

"Squeak of mice. Croak of frog. You will turn into a dog!"

"But I am a dog," said the Dog quietly, not wishing to make the Witch cross.

"Oh yes. Bother!"

"Try this instead," said the Dog. "Squeak of mice, bark of dog. You will turn into a frog!"

"Very good," croaked the Witch from under the cauldron.

The Dog had turned the Witch
into a frog, but she didn't seem to
mind too much.

They spent the night working on spells. Sometimes the Witch did spells on the Dog. Sometimes the Dog did spells on the Witch. She turned him into a banana, and

he turned her into a bone. Then she turned him into a carrot and he turned her into a donkey.

There was a nasty moment when
the donkey nearly ate the carrot.
But they had great fun all night.

"Now it's time for a ride on my
broomstick!" she cried.

"Can I come with you?" asked
the Dog. "I could do with the
fresh air."

So the Dog sat on the end of the Witch's broomstick and she said the magic words. The broomstick wobbled, but it could not get off the ground.

"You're too heavy," said the Witch. "That's why I need a cat."

"Try again, please!" begged the Dog.

"Say
the
spell
twice to
make it
stronger."
So the
Witch said
the spell twice
and it worked.
The broomstick
flew up into the
sky. The Dog sat
behind the Witch and
howled at the moon.
He felt very happy. His
tail wagged so much he
almost fell off.

When they landed back in the Witch's garden it was nearly morning.

"Time for bed! We've a busy night tomorrow," said the Witch. "It's the Grand Spell Contest!"

"Does that mean I've got the job?" asked the Dog.

"Of course!" cried the Witch. "Just make sure you switch off the cauldron before you go to bed."

CHAPTER THREE

The Dog and the Witch slept for
most of the day. When it grew
dark the Dog woke up and went
into the garden. He rolled in the
mud and walked all over the
Witch's floor. Then he did lots of

dribbles and rubbed his fur into the
carpet. The place was such a
mess! He woke the Witch by
licking her hairy chin.

"Please," said the Dog. "Before
we go to the Spell Contest, could
you take me for a walk?"

"A walk? Why do you want to
go for a walk?" asked the Witch
as she got out of bed.

"All dogs need a walk," he
replied.

"Oh very well. I need to pop
into the woods to pick some
toadstools. But we must hurry!"

So the Witch took the Dog and

they went for a walk in the woods. While they were hunting for toadstools they met Witch Cackle and her cat Sooty. They were on their way to the Grand Spell Contest.

"What are you doing with that stupid dog?" asked Cackle.

"He's a witch's dog," said the Witch. The Dog growled and Sooty leapt up a tree.

"A witch's dog? There is no

such thing as a witch's dog!"

"Oh yes, there is. And I'm taking him to the Grand Spell Contest."

"You can't take a dog to the Grand Spell Contest! It's against the rules!"

"Is it?" said the Witch.

"Yes! It says so in the Rule Book. They will throw you out!" Cackle gave a horrible laugh. "Come along, Sooty, we must hurry!"

Sooty jumped on to Cackle's shoulder and the two of them rushed off.

"That's funny. I didn't know there were any rules for the Grand Spell Contest," said the Witch.

"I bet that witch is lying," said the Dog. "Come on, let's go."

"Oh no," said the Witch. "I can't take you to the contest if it's against the rules. Anyway, all the other witches will laugh at me. Cackle was right. There is no such thing as a witch's dog."

The Witch took the Dog
home. She put on her tallest hat
and her long black gloves. She
picked up her spell-book and a
bag of worms for her spells. The
Dog watched her get ready,
feeling very sad.

"I'm very sorry, but you
must go," the Witch told the
Dog. "I'll have to get a cat
instead. Goodbye . . ."

"Goodbye," said the Dog. The Witch got on her broomstick and flew off to the Grand Spell Contest. Tears ran down the Dog's furry nose. Why couldn't he be a witch's dog? Life was very unfair!

CHAPTER FOUR

The Dog was very upset. He had
grown to love the Witch, and he
loved doing magic spells. He did
not want to go back to living on
the streets. It was warm in the

Witch's house with the cauldron
boiling away all night. And she
liked dirt and mud around the
place. It was the perfect home
for a dog . . . But he knew he had
to go.

Then he saw something on the
table. It was the Witch's wand!
She had gone to the Grand Spell
Contest without it.

"Oh no! She must have her
wand!" cried the Dog. There
was only one thing to do.

He put the wand in his mouth
and ran off.

The Dog was glad the Witch
never washed and was very smelly.
He was able to follow her trail all
the way to the Grand Spell Contest.

He arrived just in time. The
Witch was standing by the
cauldron, just about to do her
best spell.

"Hurry up!" cried the Bad
Fairy who was judging the
contest.

"Oh dear, oh dear," said the Witch, looking in her bag and in the pockets of her dress. "I have forgotten my wand!"

All the other witches laughed at her. "No cat, no wand! She's not a real witch at all!" they shouted.

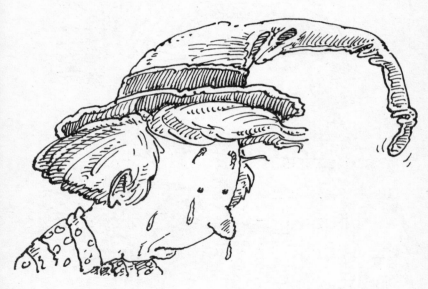

The Witch started to cry. Large dirty tears rolled down her cheeks. The witches laughed even more.

Then the Dog rushed in with the
wand in his mouth. He dropped it
at the Witch's feet.

"Thank you, thank you!" cried
the Witch. "Now I can do my
spell!"

"Wait!" said Cackle. "Stop the
contest! Throw that witch out!
Witch's dogs are against the rules!"

The other witches cheered and
waved their wands.

"What rules?" said the Bad
Fairy. "There are no rules!"

"See – I knew she was lying,"
said the Dog. He growled at
Cackle and Sooty. All the other

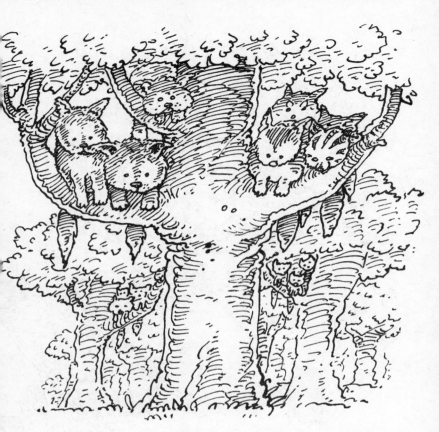

witches' cats were terrified. They
ran into the wood and hid up the
trees.

"Come back!" shouted the
witches.

The Witch and her Dog did
their best spells. The Witch

turned the Dog into a banana and
the Dog turned the Witch into a
bone. The Witch turned the Dog
into a carrot and the Dog turned
the Witch into a donkey. The
carrot kept well away from the

donkey this time and everything went perfectly.

None of the cats would come down from the trees. So the other witches had to do their spells without any help. All the spells went wrong, and Cackle did the

worst spell of all. The Bad Fairy
gave First Prize to the Witch and
her dog. It was a brand new
cauldron.

Just as the Witch was loading
her broomstick, Cackle came up.

"Where did you find that
witch's dog?" asked Cackle

"That's my secret," said the
Witch.

"I was thinking, I might get a dog," said Cackle.

"Me too," said another witch.

"I fancy a black poodle," said another.

The Witch smiled at the Dog with her black, crooked teeth.

"Shall we go?" she said.

The broomstick was so heavy that it would not lift off the ground.

"Say the magic words three times to make the spell stronger," said the Dog.

So the Witch said the magic words three times and the broomstick flew into the sky. The Dog sat proudly behind the Witch with the new cauldron on his lap.

He gave a loud, wild howl at the moon. At last he had a new home and a new job. And there was no better job in the world than being a witch's dog.

THE END